Where Is This Place?

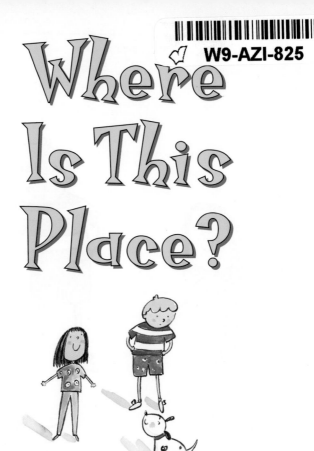

by Roz Haddle
illustrated by Amanda Haley

Harcourt

Orlando   Boston   Dallas   Chicago   San Diego

Visit *The Learning Site!*

www.harcourtschool.com

What is this? Where is this
place? Not a thing is here!

"Let's fill this place," they
say to each other. "Let's
get brushes."

Together, they sketch a yard.
They sketch a nice house in
the middle.

"Boggle, you silly pup!"
chuckles Pat. The kids
chuckle to each other.

Boggle has a nice place
to rest. He wiggles in.

"Let's sketch a school,"
says Carla. "That's simple,
don't you think?"

Pat and Carla share that task.
They talk as they sketch, but
it is not simple.

"This takes forever," grumbles
Pat. He cannot smile.

Now school is set up. "How about some friends to share it with?" asks Carla.

"Great," says Pat. The kids
sketch and talk together. What
is possible in this school?

Lots of things are possible.
Purple turtles! Bubbles that
sparkle! What a great place!